The Adventures of Nathan & Nyashia

by

Jennifer Lenny

MAPLE
PUBLISHERS

The Adventures of Nathan & Nyashia

Author: Jennifer Lenny

Copyright © Jennifer Lenny (2025)

The right of Jennifer Lenny to be identified as author of this work has been asserted by the author in accordance with section 77 and 78 of the Copyright, Designs and Patents Act 1988.

First Published in 2025

ISBN 978-1-83538-733-7 (Paperback)
    978-1-83538-734-4 (E-Book)

Book Cover, Illustrations and Layout by:
    White Magic Studios
    www.whitemagicstudios.co.uk

Published by:
    Maple Publishers
    Fairbourne Drive, Atterbury,
    Milton Keynes,
    MK10 9RG, UK
    www.maplepublishers.com

A CIP catalogue record for this title is available from the British Library.

The book is a work of fiction. Unless otherwise indicated, all the names, characters, places and incidents are either the product of the author's imagination or used in a fictitious manner. Any resemblance to actual people living or dead, events or locales is entirely coincidental, and the Publisher hereby disclaims any responsibility for them.

All rights reserved. No part of this book may be reproduced or translated by any form or by any means, electronic or mechanical, including photocopying, recording or by any information storage and retrieval system without written permission from the author.

The Adventures of Nathan and Nyashia

– by Jennifer Lenny

Other books to look out for, by Jennifer Lenny (author).

One is on Discoveries of Black Inventors. You will learn about times and events that shaped our world.

Tyrone and Tyra World of Discovery of Black Inventors

Now available on paperback & also on e-book.

ISBN 978-1-83538-130-4 (Paperback)

978-1-83538-131-1 (E-Book).

Also available is Tyrone and Tyra – Black Kings and Queens of Historical times (part 2) by Jennifer Lenny.

ISBN 978-1-83538-184-7(Paperback)

978-1-83538-185-4 (E-Book).

Another book from the same author Jennifer Lenny is – Michael and Michelle, a Welsh experience (part 2).

ISBN 978-1-83538-333-9 (Paperback)

978-1-83538-334-6 (E-Book)

Another book from the same author Jennifer Lenny is – Michael and Michelle – a Caribbean experience.

ISBN 978-1-83538-208-0 (Paperback)

978-1-83538-209-7 (E-Book).

This book is Dedicated to my beautiful granddaughter Ellexus

CONTENTS

Chapter 1

Diamond Street

It was the summer of 2025. The summer breeze had brought out most of the residents from their homes to join the activities which were taking place on their street. There were the workers of 9 to 5 washing their cars, getting them ready for the next time they needed to use them. They gleamed just like the morning sun as they washed and polished their pride and joy.

There was music being played on the street by the younger generation as they got their barbeques going, and everyone having a great time dancing to the vibe of the summer tunes being played. The older generation grandpas and grandmas sat on their porch and watched the world go by as they reminisced about the great times they used to have during the summer seasons. The small children joined a queue to buy their favourite ice-creams and ice lollies from the Toni Belle ice-cream van, while other residents cut their over grown grass which stood out from the rest.

At number 28 and 49 lived Nathan and Nyashia, they were boyfriend and girlfriend. A mixed-race couple. They have known each other since junior school. They even went to university together and had graduated at the same time. They would soon be on their travels. Nathan and Nyashia had plans to travel to a few romantic destinations starting with the Maldives in mind. Nathan was white with blond hair and wore glasses while Nyashia was mixed race with curly, long hair. She always wore a red ribbon in her hair. This was her favourite colour, and they were both 24 years old.

They decided that they should start doing some research on their favourite destinations as time would soon be upon them. They were invited to the barbeque on their street where they would get that time to enjoy themselves for the last time with their friends. Oh, what great fun they were having dancing to all their favourite tunes, laughing and joking in the mix.

The Maldives would be a great place for their first stop. Their best friends, Brad and Brandy, would miss them very much as they too have been friends since junior school.

"What do you imagine the Maldives to look like, Brandy?" asked Nyashia, as they sat down to have something to eat and drink.

Brandy replied, "I imagine crystal blue waters and sandy white beaches, the amazing sunset that you see in the glossy magazines."

"Yes, that would be just as I imagine it to be also." Nyashia agreed.

Brad and Brandy were brother and sister, and have lived on Diamond Street for many years. They just couldn't imagine living anywhere else. Everyone was having a great time as they always do at this time of year. It was getting rather late, the party had been amazing, and the organisers were packing all their equipment away. It's been a long day, and everyone was feeling tired at this point. Tomorrow would be another day.

Chapter 2

The Maldives, here we come.

The day had finally arrived, and Nathan and Nyashia were all packed and ready to travel. They said goodbye to their parents, and also to their best friends. They promised to stay in touch throughout their travels. Their transport to the airport was waiting at the door. The couple was very excited and looking forward to their trip. Mum and dad, and their best friends, Brad and Brandy, had got up early that morning to see them off as they would greatly be missed.

"Don't forget to keep in touch," Brandy hollered. The couple gave their mum and dad a big hug. Nathan said goodbye to his best friend, Brad. Then, it was time to enter the taxi.

The taxi driver drove off towards the airport.

"Hello," the taxi driver said to Nathan and Nyashia when they entered the taxi. "My name is Earlan, it's going to be quite a long drive this morning to the airport. You might want to get comfortable for the journey." Earlan handed the couple a bottle of cold water each to drink.

"Many thanks," the couple said as they received their bottles of water. "This will come in very handy."

"So, where are you travelling to?" Earlan asked the couple.

"We are off to the Maldives," Nathan and Nyashia replied.

"What beautiful destination awaits!" Earlan responded.

As the couple travelled into the early hours of the morning, they both fell asleep. The journey was quite a long one. Nyashia was first to wake up.

"Where are we?" Nyashia asked Earlan.

"We are not too far away from the airport," Earlan replied.

They were still on the motorway. Nyashia could see the sign which read '15 miles to Heathrow airport'.

"Not long now," Earlan mentioned.

"Time to wake up Nathan," Nyashia said to Earlan.

Nathan woke up with tired eyes, rubbing them very hard to clear his vision. As he looked through the window, he could see that it had been raining, also there was quite a strong wind. The branches of the trees were blowing backwards and forwards as the rain came down. They had finally arrived at the airport. It was now time to collect all their luggage from the boot of the taxi. Earlan wished them a safe journey, and the couple entered the airport.

Chapter 3

Up and away

"What terminal do we need to find, now that we are in the airport?" Nyashia asked Nathan.

"Let's have a look at my phone," Nathan replied. "We need to find terminal 3," looking at his phone.

The couple had found the terminal. It was now time to check in (fast track), then relax at the coffee shop. Nyashia wanted to check out the duty free before boarding the flight. There were lots of people travelling at this time of year. Children were also off from school which made the airport extra busy.

"I will not be long at the duty-free," Nyashia told Nathan as she went through the entrance of the duty-free shop.

Nyashia went over to the perfume section of the duty free to see if they had her favourite perfume so that she could purchase a small bottle. There stood on the shelf was her favourite bottle of perfume, *I am queen* by Lattafa. She also went over to the men's section to purchase a bottle of men's scent for Nathan – *Savage* by Dior.

Nathan was checking the announcement board to find what gate they had to attend. They had just 15 minutes to go before the gates opened.

"Have you got everything that you need?" Nathan asked.

"Yes, I have got everything that I need," Nyashia replied.

"We have run out of time for the coffee shop," Nathan said. "It's now time to check in at the gate."

The couple made their way to gate number 6. There was a long queue of excited passengers waiting to board the flight to the Maldives. The security checked their passports before entering the aircraft. They were all set to go.

The couple found their seats by numbers and made themselves comfortable. "I have a surprise for you," Nyashia said as she handed over a small package.

Nathan smiled and said, "Thank you."

As he opened the package, he could see that was his favourite scent.

"Savage," he shouted. "What a lovely surprise!" and gave Nyashia a big hug.

Once everyone was seated the pilot announced that the passengers needed to fasten their seat belts and prepare for take-off. When they were in the air the hostess came round with a trolley offering snacks and drinks and souvenirs for sale. There was also a programme of films to view. The couple looked at the programme on offer and found something that took their interest. 'Mufasa, the Lion King' was showing.

"Let's watch this one," Nathan said as he scrolled down the list of films.

"What is this film about?" Nyashia asked.

"It's about discovering who you are and the path you're meant to take."

"Sounds good to me, let's watch it," she said.

The couple made themselves cosy and got absorbed. The story line was very fascinating, exciting. "That was very exciting and adventurous," they agreed, as the movie came to an end.

It was now time for the air hostess to serve afternoon tea and sell gifts and other items that were placed on her trolley for sale.

"It will not be too long now," the air hostess said to the couple as she handed them over a tray of cakes and delicious sandwiches.

"Can't wait to land," Nyashia said to Nathan. "It's such a long flight."

At this point the couple had been on the flight for the best part of 9 hours. The total time to reach their destination to Velena International Airport would take a good long 10 hours and 20 minutes.

Sitting in front of the couple on their flight were two young men. They were friends travelling together. Their names were Raj and Lee. They were travelling to the Maldives for the first time. Raj was an Indian man, and Lee was Chinese. They had made friends with the couple on the flight and had exchanged contact numbers as they would be staying at the same bungalow on their arrival.

The pilot of the aircraft had made an announcement that the aeroplane would be making a landing in 15 minutes. The aircraft lights had lit up, showing to buckle up. Nyashia looked out of her tiny aircraft window. There in front of her she could see the landmark of this beautiful building, the Hukuru Miskiy (Friday Mosque).

"Have a look through the window," Nyashia said to Nathan, "I can see the landmark, we are almost there."

Nathan took a look through the tiny window and could see the landmark.

Nathan asked Nyashia, "Did you know that the mosque is a testament to the Maldivian history and architecture?"

"No, I didn't know this," Nyashia replied.

"It was built in 1656."

"Very interesting," she said.

The aircraft was ready for touch down; they had a safe landing.

Chapter 4

Welcome to the Maldives

It was now time to find their carousel number and pick up their luggage. Their transport was waiting to take them to their bungalow. They would have to go over by either seaplane, speedboat, or domestic flight. The couple decided that they would travel by seaplane as the experience would give a full view of the atolls. (The atolls are groups of islands and reefs that surround a lagoon). There are 26 natural atolls of the Maldives. The Maldives is a small country located in the Indian Ocean formed by 26 natural atolls that have been further divided into several administrative units.

The Maldives enjoys a tropical climate with warm sunshine throughout the year making it a place for divers and snorkellers with beautiful turquoise sea. Steeped in history, it weaves together vibrant Indian, Sri Lankan and Arab culture creating a unique tapestry of beautiful heritage. The Maldives is the flattest country in the world with an average ground level of just 1.5 metres (around 5 feet) above sea level. It's made up of 1,190 coral islands and is famous for its crystal clear waters and luxurious overwater bungalows, tropical beaches with white sand and palm trees, awaiting your arrival.

The couple had to be checked in for their seaplane flight. Their bags and luggage were the right weight in kilogrammes, 5 kilogrammes for hand luggage and 20 kilogrammes for their main luggage. They were then escorted to a lounge where they could relax ahead of their seaplane journey.

"I can't believe that we are finally here," Nyashia said to Nathan in excitement.

"Yes, what great fun we will have now that we are here," Nathan replied.

After a cold drink they were called to board the seaplane. They found their seats and sat down. Boarding a seaplane was relatively straight forward. It was time to take off as the pilot wasted no time once everyone was boarded. The taking off on the seaplane was really an interesting experience – it was noisy, bumpy but totally worth it as the scenery the couple experienced from their tiny windows en route was astonishing. They got to view small islands, remote desert islands and beautiful waters.

"This journey is a once in a lifetime experience," Nyashia said to Nathan, "I can't wait to start our holiday."

"Can't wait," Nathan replied.

It was now time to step off the flight. The warm tropical sea and air felt inviting as the couple set foot off the seaplane. This was going to be the beginning of a great adventure.

Chapter 5

Time to Explore

The following day, as they walked along the seashore, Nathan found a shiny object just sitting there on the sand. As he picked it up to have a closer look, he could see that it looked like an ankh (key of life).

"Look, what I've found," he said to Nyashia.

"That's lucky, imagine finding an ankh (key of life) just sitting there on the beach. Maybe someone might have lost it," Nyashia said.

"I will just hold on to it for the time being," Nathan responds.

As they continued their walk, they met up with their newfound friends, Raj and Lee. They were also going for a stroll.

"Let's go over to the lounge chairs with the parasols," Nyashia said to the others.

"Great idea," everyone said.

As they made themselves comfortable on the lounge chairs, a waiter came over to take their orders for drinks. They were handed a menu with lots of exotic cocktails and snacks.

"What are you going to have?" Nathan asked the group.

"I'm going to have the Tropical Ocean with some ice," Nyashia said.

"I think I will have the same as you," Nathan said.

Raj and Lee picked the Blue Lagoon from the menu. The waiter took their orders and off he went to get their drinks.

"Tell us a bit about yourselves," Raj asked the couple.

Nathan answered with a surprising grin. "Well, myself and Nyashia, we have known each other all our lives. We live on the same street in the UK

(United Kingdom), we went to the same school, and we have just graduated from university and are now qualified schoolteachers. How about you?"

"I was born in India and was brought up by my grandfather as my parents went to live in another country for work when I was very young. When my grandfather passed away, he left me a magic carpet, and this carpet was to bring me good luck. This carpet can fly and whenever I'm sad I go for a ride, and I feel a lot better on my return. It can also be used for many different things. One day when I was flying around, I saw some boys picking on my friend Lee and I flew down from my magic carpet to rescue him. This is how we became good friends."

"Oh, I see," Nathan said.

"How about your story?" Nyashia asked Lee.

"Well, my story is very much different from Raj's. When I was growing up in school I was always being picked on, so I went to martial arts school to learn how to fight. I learned to use the nunchucks."

"What are the nunchucks?" Nyashia asked.

Lee explained, "It's 2 sticks connected by a rope or chain. It enhances martial art skills. It enables the development of quick hand movements and improves posture. I was born in China and moved to the UK at the age of 12."

The waiter had now arrived with the drinks.

"Thank you," the group, said as the waiter passed the drinks around on a round tray.

"Help yourselves to snacks," the waiter said as he passed the snacks around on the tray.

"This drink is so nice and refreshing," Nyashia said as she took a sip.

The resort that the group was staying on was called the Siyam world resort. It's a 5-star Maldivian resort, the biggest in the Maldives. It's a place for anyone looking for adventure with a huge water park. With a 4-kilometre sandy beach, you can walk around this island in just 60 minutes, taking the sand between your toes with beautiful scenery and palm trees. There are small pathways taking you around the island, with every part of the island giving you a unique part of paradise.

"Well, what's our plans for tomorrow?" Nathan asked the group.

"We have got a lot of choices. We can go jet skiing, kayaking, deep sea diving, laze around on a hammock, sit in a jacuzzi or go for a long ride on a hired bike, just to name a few," Nyashia said, "the choice is ours and it's all set within a serene surrounding."

"How about starting the day at the underwater restaurant for breakfast?" Raj said.

"Great idea!" the group agreed.

"9 o'clock sharp. Jolly good," Nathan said.

Then they all made their way to their luxury bungalows.

Chapter 6

Another day in Paradise.

The group met at the underwater restaurant for breakfast.

"Good morning, everyone," Nyashia said as they sat down for breakfast.

"Good morning, Nyashia," the others responded.

"This is lovely," she said. "Imagine dining in an ethereal world surrounded by the ocean's finest colourful coral reefs, schools of tropical fish and even the occasional shark?"

"It's nice in here," Raj commented.

The restaurant was like being in a giant glass fishbowl. There were glass windows everywhere with colourful fishes swimming all around. The ambience, the unique settings and once in a lifetime experience transcends the mere label 'restaurant'.

"Stunning underwater views," Raj commented.

The waiter was on his way with the menu.

"Good morning, everyone. My name is Jerome. I have two menus for you this morning, one for food the other for drinks."

Jerome passed around the menus.

"Have you visited the Maldives before?" he asked.

"It's the first time for all of us," Nathan replied.

"I'm sure you will enjoy your stay here," Jerome said, "welcome."

Pricing for breakfast commenced at $250 per person. The individual breakfast menu boasted an expansive selection ranging from a revitalising champagne option to an array of egg preparations and freshly squeezed

oranges. Everyone gave their order to Jerome and off he went, sure to return shortly. While waiting for their order the group talked about what they were going to do after breakfast, maybe a trip to the water parks would be nice or going to a live performance whatever their choice, it was sure to be enjoyable. Before they knew it their breakfast had arrived. Jerome was very good at his job and had delivered a great service. Everyone was handed their breakfast and order of drinks. They thanked Jerome for the service. What great way to begin the day, with much indulgence! Welcome to paradise.

Chapter 7

Deep sea diving

After breakfast the group had decided to go deep sea diving. They hooked up with the holiday rep and booked it. There were many great options to choose from. While they were in the Maldives deep sea diving had to be first on their list of things to do. The group was about to undertake a luxurious couple of days exploring the breath-taking reefs and atolls of the Maldives above and beneath the waves and uncover hidden natural wonders. Raj and Lee met up with Nathan and Nyashia at their bungalow and then everyone made their way to meet their diving instructor for their first ever diving lesson. They were taken by boat to join their catamaran (boat) where they would be staying for the next few days.

"Good morning, everyone," their diving instructor said, with a big smile. "My name is Danny, and I will be your diving instructor for the next few days. Today we will be getting up close to giant Manta rays, uncover shipwrecks and witness the apex predators of the ocean. An entirely new layer of excitement to this underwater world. Drawing in massive pelagic creatures that are anything, but shy. Sharks make multiple appearances and there are plenty of them. Please don't be nervous as you will be guided every step of the way."

Previous to this the group had been taken to a swimming pool for training so that they could prepare for their ocean diving experience. In this pool they were able to practise for their big day ahead.

"Is everyone ready?" Danny the diving instructor asked.

"Yes," everyone said.

Now it was time to explore. As they entered the water and dived backwards into the sea, they were instantly confronted by giant blotched fantail stingrays and pink whiprays. Once they were in the waters it was so relaxing. Colourful fishes swam past them as they went deeper into the deep clear waters. They were able to take an underwater camera to record every moment of this great experience. Their underwater time slot had now expired. Tomorrow they would be checking out some of the other atolls, moving along and exploring more, their instructor explained, once everyone was back on the catamaran safely.

"That was a great experience!" Nathan said to Nyashia once they were back on board.

"It sure was," Nyashia said. "How was it for you, Raj and Lee?"

"It was like no other," Raj said.

"Fantastic," agreed Lee. "I'm happy for the experience."

It was now time for something to eat and drink on board their luxury accommodation.

"Compliments to the chief," the group said as they finished their delightful meal.

They decided to retire as they had to rise early for another adventure under the sea.

"Goodnight, everyone," Nathan said, "See you in the morning."

Raj and Lee said, "Goodnight, see you in the morning," and off they all went to get some rest.

Chapter 8

Time to explore some more...

The group got up very early the next morning, had breakfast on board their luxury catamaran. The chef had prepared a nice breakfast for them, a healthy breakfast to start the day, as they would be spending a couple of hours under water. The group was again instructed by their diving instructor the correct way to put on their oxygen tanks, just a short briefing on health and safety then they were all ready to explore.

The second dive was a little bit farther away from the last one the day before. They were now about to explore a different atoll. Nathan was hoping to take some great underwater footage with his water camera. While they were in the waters, they discovered beautiful, coloured fishes, black and white with orange fins. They were now in the reef, the local name is Lanken. They also encountered a giant Manta ray. These graceful ocean giants gather in large numbers at cleaning stations where they arrive to be groomed by tiny cleaner fish like Rasses and Gobies which remove parasites and dead skin. These natural spa treatment helps Manta stay healthy. (The group was later told this by their diving instructor once their experience was over).

The Manta looked like a giant bat flapping its fins as it swam around in full circle. The group was surrounded by schools of trigger fish and yellowtail snapper as they explored a bit farther. There were lots of rocks with different colourful fishes coming from around the rocks and what seemed to look like caves. A Holhola Thila is a stunning underwater pinnacle in the Maldives renowned for its dramatic overhangs, vibrant soft coral, and thriving marine biodiversity. (The word Thila refers to submerged coral towers and caves). The group even got to explore the wreck. (Mirando Fesdhoo wreck). Every encounter with a giant Manta felt like a spiritual experience with this one leading the group disciples to the wonderous wreck of Fesdhoo. While still exploring Nyashia saw what she thought to be a mermaid in the water. The mermaid had a black face with a friendly smile, long black hair with a long, big tail, it had a nice spirit. Nyashia could feel its presence before it just disappeared. That night while sleeping she saw the mermaid in her sleep. The mermaid told her not to be afraid as she would protect her, then disappeared. Nyashia woke out of sleep in a cold sweat, shaking and wondering why she had such a dream, and this would have been once too often that this mermaid had presented herself. The following day Nyashia told Nathan about her dream.

"I wonder why you had this dream?" Nathan said.

"Time will tell," Nyashia replied.

Chapter 9

Mami Wata (The black mermaid)

What does it mean to dream about Mami Wata? Men and women say that they first saw her in a dream. A beautiful woman with long black hair. Sometimes holding a mirror and always near water, an ocean, a river or by a bathroom sink. The dream feels real. The air is heavy and smells like salt. You can feel her eyes on you. She might smile, or she might say nothing at all. One thing is always true, when you wake up you cannot forget her and if it happens more than once, she may have chosen you. They say a mysterious mermaid lives in the ocean/river (water). She's half woman half fish with flowing hair, golden jewellery and eyes as deep as the water. Some say she brings fortune beauty and healing to those who honour her, others fear her saying that she drags people into the underwater world never to return. Fishermen still bring her gifts – mirrors, perfume and coins, but betray her and she vanishes taking your peace with her, she is more than a myth. Shrines still stand in her name across the African and the diaspora cultures. She is still a much talked about aspect of global culture offering inspiration to practitioners of art, music and literature. Historically, scholars trace her origin to early encounters between Europeans and West Africans in the 15th century. In African and Afro-Caribbean myth, Mami Wata has been rendered as a saviour figure and symbol of fortune. She is often depicted as a beautiful seductive mermaid-like figure associated with wealth, beauty and spiritual powers. She is sometimes depicted with a snake around her neck which represents both divinity and the art of divination. Somewhere beneath the sea the spirit of Mami Wata is always watching.

Chapter 10
The glowing beach

Nathan and Nyashia were looking for something different to experience while visiting the Maldives. Off they went to see their resort representative to find out what was on offer. The resort representative told Nathan and Nyashia about the glowing beach. This would be something different to explore.

"Spending a night at the glowing beach is one of my favourites," he said. "This experience is selling very quickly and is most popular among visitors. There is a beach that glows at night. You really can't afford to miss this place as it offers an otherworldly experience. There is a beach in Motu Island, it's also known as Vaadhoo Island that glows at night. The glow in the dark basically is a natural phenomenon called bioluminescence where light is emitted or created by a living organism. The beach is a part of Vaadhoo Island which is one of the islands of the raw atoll in the Maldives."

There was excitement written all over his face. "It's a small gem of Maldives but in recent times it has become one of the topmost sought after places."

"Let's book it," Nathan said to Nyashia.

"Sounds good to me," Nyashia said.

"Be here tonight at 8 pm sharp, for transfers," their representative told them.

The couple went away, very excited about this new adventure. They spent the day just thinking about their newfound adventure. They couldn't wait to tell their friends, Raj and Lee. They might want to join them on this adventure. Raj and Lee had decided to book up for the trip as this was something that they had never experienced before. The group spent the day just lazing at the bar drinking non-alcoholic cocktails talking about past and present holidays. Raj and Lee were well travelled and had knowledge of different countries

around the world. This adventure would be one of many.

On arrival at the beach, it was dark, and everything stood still including the waters. As Nathan and Nyashia walked along the seashore with Raj and Lee there was a sudden glow on the sand. It was a golden lamp just sitting there, as if it was waiting to be rescued by a passer-by. It shone bright under the moon light. Nathan picked it up and rubbed it as it was covered in sand and it seemed to have been there for a while. He rubbed it until all the sand disappeared. Then within a blink of an eye a puff of smoke came from inside the lamp. Nyashia, Raj and Lee looked with widened eyes. They could not believe what they had just witnessed. It looked as if a genie had appeared right in front of them.

"Hello," a voice spoke from behind the puff of smoke.

As it cleared the group could see a tall figure in the moonlight.

"My name is Omar," the voice said as the smoke cleared quickly. "I am here to grant you three wishes. You must take me with you as you might need me soon," he said with a clear echoing voice. The group stood in front of him looking very puzzled.

Nyashia asked Omar, in dismay, "Why will we be needing you soon?"

"I'm here to help you," Omar said. "I'm your trusted friend and I will grant you 3 wishes of anything you ask but for now you need to keep me safe."

He then disappeared back into the lamp.

"That was so surreal," Raj said to the others.

Nathan placed the lamp in his rucksack. He would take it back with him to the bungalow. The waters turned a glow of blue as the group walked along the shore. It was like nothing they had ever seen. The waves flowed back and forth to the shore. They walked along the sand which glowed a colourful blue as they left their footprints in the sand. They were now being called by their holiday representative. Their time on the adventure was now over and what an adventure...

Chapter 11

The day after....

The following day Nathan and Nyashia got up very early to meet up with Raj and Lee for breakfast. They visited the underwater restaurant. They had spoken about last night's adventure on the glowing beach. They tried to make sense of what they had experienced while on the beach that night and the lamp that Nathan had found on the sand. Omar had given them food for thought –maybe there is a lot more to the Maldives that meet the eye? Or was it all a dream? It had to be real as Nathan had the lamp in his procession as proof of what had taken place that night.

"What do you think the genie meant when he said that we will be needing him soon," Nyashia questioned.

The others tried to put the puzzle together in the best way that they could.

"Maybe this place is a magical place," Raj said.

"I wonder what surprise awaits us," Lee added, as he scratched his head waiting for an answer. Nyashia decided to share her dream with Raj and Lee about the black mermaid that she saw not once but twice, the first time in the water when they went diving a few days ago. Raj and Lee were silent as they listened to Nyashia's claims.

"A black mermaid?" Raj asked Nyashia.

" Yes!" Nyashia said as she too tried to make clarity of it all.

"Omar said we have three wishes, do you think that we can get him to tell us with just one wish," Nathan asked the group.

"I think we should wait a while as we don't want to waste our wishes. We might need them for more important things," Raj said.

"I wonder if we called upon Omar he can tell us," Nyashia asked the group.

"That might be one of our wishes used up," Lee said, "I think we should wait a while."

The waiter came over to the table to take their orders.

"Good morning," the waiter said with a friendly smile as he handed over the menu of the day. He asked how their holiday in the Maldives was going so far.

Everyone was silent to begin with then Nathan asked him, "How long have you lived here?"

The waiter told Nathan that he had lived in the Maldives for many years.

"Are there any unusual stories that you know about that happened here?"

"Not that I can recall," the waiter answered.

The group was now back to square one, with no clues to the missing puzzle. The waiter took their orders and off he went. He later returned with their orders. After breakfast, Raj had an idea maybe they could go for a ride on his magic carpet in search – but what would they be looking for? The question remains...

Chapter 12

The magic carpet flight

After breakfast the group decided that they were going to go on a little adventure on Raj's magic carpet to see what they can discover from air level. They all got on board the magic carpet as it flew above the blue skies. They saw a beautiful view of the atolls, many different shades of blue – the water looked so beautiful from above. They saw a lot of greenery. Then suddenly Raj spotted something that looked like a human with a long tail sitting there on the rock. It looked like a black woman. He brought this to the attention of the others just in case they might have missed it.

"Did everyone just see what I thought I just saw? Could it be a mermaid?" Raj said to the others as the magic carpet got closer to the waters.

The view of what it was, became very clear or was it just their minds playing tricks on them?

"Shall we fly down," Raj said to the group "to take a closer look?"

At what they thought was a mermaid. She kept splashing her long tail in and out of the waters, her long hair floating around her like seaweed. As they flew down she just disappeared into the waters, like magic never to be seen again. The group again tried to make some sense of what they had witnessed in full view. They wished that they had the answer to what was going on around them. It all became a mystery which none of them could solve. Raj and the rest of the group decided to fly back to their bungalow as there really wasn't anything else to see. How were they going to resolve this trail of reoccurring events taking place?.....

Chapter 13

Rainy days

The following day the weather was a little different from the other days. The sun had disappeared, and the rain had come down. Thundery stormy weather had hit the Maldives with grey skies in the horizon. The group had decided that they were going to stay in their bungalows as there really wasn't much to do. Nathan and Nyashia looked at the video of their underwater experience. They talked about what Brad and Brandy their best friends would be getting up to back home in the UK. They wondered about their parents, maybe it's time to give them a call to find out how they're getting on.

"I will give mum and dad a ring now," Nyashia said as she dialled the number. "Hello mum, it's Nyashia."

"Hello. How is the holiday going?" her mum asked with a happy voice.

"We are having a whale of a time out here," Nyashia replied. "Nathan and I have made new friends, Raj and Lee. We went deep sea diving the other day, it was fantastic. We spent two days on a catamaran. We also went to a glowing beach.

"Glowing beach?" mum asked. "What was that all about?"

"You can only go there at night to really appreciate it. The sand glows the colour of blue as you walk on it. It's just amazing wish you were here."

"Sounds like you and Nathan are having a fantastic time. How about the weather?"

"Well, the weather has not been nice, today, it's raining. We are in our accommodation as it's not so nice today so I thought I would give you a buzz. How are Brad and Brandy, have you seen them lately?"

"Yes, they're doing fine and asked about you and Nathan. I told them that

I'm sure you will call soon."

"That's great, tell them that we are having lots of fun and will see them soon. Ok mum, it's now time to go. Tell Nathan's mum and dad that we called."

"I will."

"Goodbye mum, love you."

"Goodbye, love you too, take care."

"Mum will pass on the message," Nyashia said to Nathan as she put the phone down.

"Well at least everyone back home will know that we still have them all in mind," Nathan said with a smile.

Chapter 14

Horseback riding

With lots to do on Nathan and Nyashia's list of things while in the Maldives the couple decided to go horseback riding. Neither of them had been on a horse before. The stormy weather had passed, and the sun was back again. Riding was something that they always wanted to do as a couple, and had talked about it before their holiday. Early morning would be the best time as the sun would not be too hot. They met up with their riding instructor on the beach. They had a briefing to get to grips with riding their horses. Their riding instructor went through many instructions before they got on their horse. They were both given safety helmets to put on.

Their horse-riding coach was a young man by the name of Martyn. He was tall, with a slim build, dark curly hair and a very wide smile.

"Good morning," Martyn said as he passed them their safety helmets. "I will guide you every step of the way," noticing the nervous expression on Nyashia's face.

Nathan got on the horse without any help while Nyashia needed a hand to get on. Martyn was an equestrian (an expert horseback rider) the couple felt very safe with him by their side. The horses strolled slowly along the white sandy beach.

"How you feeling?" Nathan asked Nyashia as they went about their first ever ride.

"A little nervous," she said as she held on to the reins tightly with both hands. "I think I will be alright once I get the feel of being on the horse's back."

"You're doing just fine," Nathan said.

After a stroll of just 15 minutes the horse started to gallop slowly along the golden white sands. This was so amazing. The couple were so relaxed as the horses galloped some more. Nathan asked the riding coach if they were allowed to have a race just to get a better riding experience.

"Yes, of course," Martyn said.

The couple raced slowly on the horse's back.

"This is just the way I imagined it to be," Nyashia said, with the wind in her hair and the sea breeze blowing in her direction just like in the movies.

Nyashia gave her horse a soft gentle touch along his face as he slowed down. It was a beautiful white horse with a long tail. The riding experience was now over, they had both had a wonderful time.

As the couple got down from their horses their riding coach Martyn made a comment, "This will be a moment that will forever be etched in your hearts as I can see that you both have had a fantastic time."

"One that will be cherished for ever," Nyashia replied.

Chapter 15

We are off to the capital Mali of Maldives.

Today, Nathan, Nyashia, Raj and Lee will be taking a day trip to the capital city of Mali. It's a bit difficult to explore the land when one is surrounded by mesmerising waters. This trip will give them a chance to witness the actual lifestyle of the locals residing in this destination, from marvellous structures to vibrant streets. This city is truly breath-taking; they can visit the national museum if they wish, located in the Sultan park. The museum comprises enormous historical artefacts including royal artefacts, stone objects and significant antiques from Buddhist traditions. There is also a fish market where you can purchase fish at the cheapest prices. They might fancy taking a boat ride.

The Maldives also gives them a chance to have the magical experience of seeing different shades of water below as you fly over the island if you go by seaplane. The local boat is called a Dhoni. If you decide to take this trip while you're there the seaplane are twin engine float planes which take you over many atolls. From the air you get a real sense of just how isolated and beautiful the Maldivian islands really are.

The island creates a pattern in the sea as the deep ocean crashes into sand bars and coral reefs round circles of pristine white sands with centres of thick mangroves dotting the horizon many islands are surrounded by miles of shallow waters low enough to wave through at low tide. They might want to take a submarine ride. This is a popular excursion among visitors to the island. The underwater submarine ride explores the depths of the ocean for this experience. This descending adventure into the blue will show them everything from shipwrecks to sharks. A whole new world waits ahead....

Chapter 16

Nyashia is taken to the marine kingdom

Nathan and Nyashia were now on their 10th day in the Maldives enjoying everything that it has to offer. They have so far managed to do all the things that they wanted to do. In the evening they would take a stroll along the beach. They walked along the shoreline under the stars with the golden white sand between their toes and dipped their feet in the clear blue crystal waters. The breeze coming from the sea refreshed their senses. They laughed together and splashed the water on each other as they chased each other up and down the shore.

It was a time of enjoyment and relaxation time for themselves as a couple. Nyashia dipped her face in the water and enjoyed looking at the colourful fishes darting around her feet. They were on the beach for 15 minutes when suddenly, a big whale came out of the water. He had a big head with a large tail that splashed with revenge. He opened his large mouth and swallowed Nyashia in whole.

Suddenly Nyashia had vanished from the face of the earth. She had been taken. Nathan stared in dismay, he could not believe his eyes. What had just taken place? What could he do? How was he going to save her? he wondered. The love of his life had vanished in an instant. His heart was shattered into a million pieces. He ran up and down the beach calling her name 'Nyashia, Nyashia,' could she have been gone for ever? He then made his way back to the bungalow to tell Raj and Lee what had just taken place.

Raj and Lee were listening to some music just chilling on the balcony of their bungalow. Nathan rushed up to them out of breath, tears streaming down his face.

"Nyashia has been taken," he shouted as he fell to his knees.

"Taken where?" they both asked.

He told them about the whale that came out of the water and how it had swallowed her up.

"We have no time to waste," Raj said. "We must find her before it's too late."

Raj dashed to fetch his magic carpet. They all got on to the magic carpet – Nathan, Raj and Lee. They flew around the open skies looking high and low. Then suddenly Raj spotted a red ribbon floating in the water.

"Look over there," he shouted. "I can see something floating above the water."

"What is it?" Nathan shouted in excitement. "Is it her?" The magic carpet flew down to where the object was. As they got nearer they could see that it was Nyashia's red ribbon, but Nyashia was still nowhere to be seen. The search was still on....

Chapter 17

The search is on

They continued to fly around looking for more clues. In the distance they could see something that looked like a black woman sitting on a rock, combing her long black hair and she had a mirror in her hand. Could it be the black mermaid? The one that they saw a few days ago. There were big splashes coming from out of the water as she splashed her long tail in and out of the water.

"Look over there, to the right," Raj said in amazement as the magic carpet flew in the direction of where the mermaid was sitting on a big rock. "Do you see what I see? It looks like the mermaid. Let's fly down to talk to her she might know something."

The magic carpet turned in the direction that Raj wanted it to go, then it slowed down and landed next to her. They felt a strong wind ripple across the water sending a cold chill down their spine. There, in front of them, in full view was a woman unlike one they had ever seen. Her skin just shimmered like bronze under the sun. Her long hair cascading down her back in the waves. She sat on the rock.

"Hello," she said to them, in a soft voice. "I was expecting you. I'm here to help you."

She told them that she had tried to show Nyashia a few signs but somehow it was ignored.

"What is your name?" Nathan asked.

"My name is Mami Wata," she said with an inviting smile on her face, "the guardian of mysteries, the mother of the waters. I was born here so I know the sea like no other. I know where Nyashia is." "Where is she?" Nathan asked with a trembling voice.

"She has been taken to the marine kingdom. We can go there to rescue her. It's not going to be easy," she said, "but with my knowledge of the sea I can take you there. You must come back later today. We must prepare for this encounter. Come back at 6pm. Go now and prepare."

She then vanished into the water.

"We must go back to pick up a few things," Nathan said. "The magic lamp will come in handy as we have 3 wishes. Also the ankh."

"My nunchucks, as well," Lee said, "that might come in handy."

They flew back to their bungalows to prepare as time was moving on. On their arrival they started to get everything they needed together. They were happy that they had got to speak to the mermaid who was happy to help them. They kept a close eye on the time as they had to be back for 6pm.

Chapter 18

The marine kingdom, here we come

Nathan, Raj and Lee had arrived back at the spot where they had seen the mermaid. She was on time waiting for them to arrive.

"I'm going to put a spell on you," she said. "This will enable you to stay under the water for as long as it takes. Have you all prepared yourself for this adventure?"

"Yes," they all said at once.

"Then let's go."

She told them to follow her as she knew the route to where they were heading. They went deep down the ocean. As they swam, they passed a lot of tropical fishes along the way surrounded by corals and rocks, also a shipwreck. Then they came to what looked like a golden gate.

"The gate is locked," Nathan panicked as they approached it.

"Don't worry," the mermaid assured them. "I will guide you, I'm here to help. Use your key," she said to Nathan.

Nathan dug into his pocket and out came a golden key, the ankh which he had found on the beach on the first day of arrival in the Maldives.

"It works," he said in excitement with a sign of relief on his face.

They found themselves in a vast underwater palace, gold and precious gems adorned the coral walls, and strange looking creatures swam through the water like living lanterns. It was like nothing they had ever seen before. They could have sworn that they were on a movie set, but this was so surreal. Then when they least expected a sea monster came out of nowhere.

"Have you got an invitation?" he spoke with a deep uninviting voice.

It was a sea octopus. It had a big round head with two bright bulging eyes that lit up like light bulbs. Its 6 arms were covered with suckers which it used to grab who ever stood in its way. It also had 2 legs that moved in great motion around its unwanted visitors. Its arms and legs moved very swiftly, each arm containing its own mini brain. It was moving around them very viciously.

"Where do you think you're going without being invited?" he yelled.

"We have come to take Nyashia back to the land where she belongs," Nathan said to the sea octopus.

"Oh no, you're not going any farther," the octopus said with an angry voice, "you must get past me first."

The mermaid told Nathan that it was now time to call upon the genie of the lamp to help them. (time for their 1st wish). Nathan rubbed the lamp as hard as he could.

"What do you wish for? Your wish is my command," Omar's voice came out of the lamp.

"We need help," Nathan said, "we need to get past this sea octopus who is standing in our way and stopping us from going any farther."

"Firstly," Omar said, "Lee needs to put him to sleep using his martial arts skills. I will then send you a big net to tie him up. Then destroy his 3 hearts 2 of which pump blood through the gills and one which circulates oxygenated blood throughout the body."

Lee brought out his nunchucks and found himself tackling the octopus. This wasn't an easy task but he managed to put him to sleep. The octopus was out for the count as Lee and the others managed to get him in the net.

"Great work," the mermaid said, "now let's move on to the next gate."

Chapter 19

Creatures of the sea

The group had destroyed the sea octopus; it was now time to find gate number 2.

"That was heavy work," Lee told the others.

"It sure was," Raj and Nathan agreed as they followed the mermaid to the next golden gate.

"Get your key ready," the mermaid said to Nathan as they approached the golden gate. Nathan took out the key from his pocket and turned the lock.

"It's open," he said in amazement. As they all entered, they had another encounter. This time they stumbled across a huge jelly fish awaiting their arrival. It was massive, its top opened like a giant umbrella and had long strands hanging from underneath its body. The top part of the jelly fish moved in and out, up and down, and swam around them very swiftly.

"Why are you here?" it asked in a very hostile voice.

"We have come to take Nyashia back to the land to which she belongs," Nathan said.

"Well, if I were you," the jelly fish said, "I would go back, never to return, as Nyashia is safe here." "Looks like we have another challenge," the mermaid said.

The mermaid told the group a little bit about the jelly fish as this task to get him out of the way would be easier than the first challenge that they had with the sea octopus.

"The jelly fish has no brains, bones, and heart," the mermaid informed the group, "instead they have a nerve network which is distributed throughout their bodies allowing them to sense their environment and react accordingly.

The box jelly fish are the most venomous marine animals in the world. Jelly fish stings are a common fear so we must be very careful."

Then suddenly, a group, a bloom of jelly fish appeared circling them, so they were unable to move out of the circle, they were trapped. The mermaid told Nathan that it was time to call upon Omar, the genie in the lamp, for a second wish. Nathan rubbed the magic lamp once again and the genie's voice appeared.

"What do you wish for?" said Omar. "Your wish is my command."

"We have a problem here with a giant jelly fish. He won't let us go any farther," Nathan said. "He is blocking our path."

"Leave him to me," Omar said.

The genie was able to dismantle him very quickly, and tricked him as he had no brains. The jelly fish was also put to sleep and they were all free to continue their search for Nyashia.

Chapter 20

The final hurdle

The group was now able to continue with their search. As the jelly fish too was put to sleep there was no stopping them. They had entered 2 gates and now onto the 3rd gate.

"Does anyone need a break?" the mermaid asked.

"No," Nathan said, "we must continue. Nyashia must be saved."

Deep in the ocean in the cold darkness lurks a mysterious ancient creature. The vampire squid lives at depths below 600 metres, a depth range where oxygen tends to be depleted. It has 8 legs and is 12ins long, the size of a (football). It is found in tropical seas. This creature has the largest eyes in the world.

"Who invited you?" the group heard a voice echo as they entered the 3rd gate.

The vampire squid sounded just like a hostile creature from the twilight zone. The group could not believe what they were up against. With its deep red colour, icy blue eyes, and webbed tentacles that resembled a cape, the vampire squid appeared quite frightening, illuminated by its bioluminescent glow against the inky darkness of the deep sea. It moved very swiftly around them with its eyes always stuck on them. Then suddenly the group witnessed more than one. They were now surrounded.

"They occupy territories in the sea," the mermaid told them as the group felt boxed in. They were now at the headquarters of the sea and very much in danger. They were in the enemy's occupied territory.

"They represent powers of chaos," the mermaid said. "These principalities will seek to stop us, but we will get Nyashia out safe. They cannot stop us, we have to keep going, they cannot prevail against the powers of Omar the genie. We must call upon him for help. We will move forward, we will be given clear direction to dismantle them if we wish. They will lose their influence over their territories.”

“Why are you here?” the vampire squid asked for the second time.

“We are here to take Nyashia back to the land where she belongs,” Nathan answered in a very angry voice.

“You must get past me first,” the vampire squid said.

The body of the vampire squid opened like a pineapple. The squid then drew its webbed tentacles up and over them. It was now time for defence. It revealed its sharp looking spines in an attempt to attack.

“We must defend ourselves,” the mermaid shouted as she hit the leader of the vampire with her long fish tail and sent him sailing over to the other side of the waters. Then Lee hit the rest of his cronies with his nunchucks. They were all put to sleep this time without the help of Omar, the genie. They still had one wish left. It was time to continue their search as the vampire squids were all dismantled.

Chapter 21

Nyashia is found

The group was now past the vampire squids and they found themselves in another room. This room had lots of glass tanks with all sorts of people stuck inside them. The names of the people were on the glass tank on a plaque. They read – Veronica, Cynthia, Lorraine, Valerie, Nyomi, Ellexus, Natalie, and Nyashia.

"I found her," Nathan shouted in excitement, as they swam around the tanks looking at the names written on the front.

"Use your key," the mermaid said as she flashed her long tail towards the entrance of the keyhole. Nyashia looked in shock, surprise, happiness and joy all at once when she saw that it was Nathan coming to the rescue. She was stuck in a huge water tank sitting on a throne just like a princess.

"The lock works," Nathan said as he opened the tank door with the golden key.

Nyashia was now free, it was time to get her back to her land. All of a sudden, a big cloud of darkness appeared in front of them. It was the whale, the one that had swallowed her in full and had taken her to the marine kingdom.

"Why are you here?" the whale said in an angry voice.

"We are here to take Nyashia back to the land where she belongs. There will be no stopping us now that we are here," Nathan said.

"Hold on to my tail," the mermaid said to Nyashia. "And get ready for action," to the others.

Lee had his nunchucks in his hand and swung it so hard that it hit the whale in one eye. He was unable to attack as he tried to stop the rescue. He was weak on his own as all his bodyguards were put to sleep.

He sat on his throne shouting, "You best come back," as the group fled from the scene.

The whale was the prince of the sea. And Nyashia – he wanted her to be his wife, the princess of the sea. This was the reason why Nyashia was taken. This was never going to happen anytime soon as the search party never gave up until they found her.

The mermaid took the group back to where she had met them. The magic carpet was there waiting for Raj to give instructions for their get-away.

"Thank you," Nathan said to the mermaid, "for helping us out."

"We have all played a great part in the rescue. You must go now," she said.

The group got on the magic carpet and away it flew in the right direction Raj directed it to fly. They waved goodbye to the mermaid and she wished them luck. With little time left before their return to the UK, it was now time to pack their bags. Time to return home…

Chapter 22

Holiday is over

Nathan and Nyashia were on the aeroplane. Their holiday had come to an end. As Nathan sat next to Nyashia on the aeroplane not a word was spoken between them. It was time to gather their thoughts, the whole holiday in general. Nathan was thinking about the role that he played in the rescuing of Nyashia. He was brave and courageous just like Mufasa, the Lion King. It was all about discovering who you are and the path you're meant to take. Meanwhile, Nyashia looked through the tiny window of the aeroplane. She could see the sea which sparkled under the sun. The ocean, sky and sea seemed silent. Was it all a dream? she thought. Or just a great adventure? Nathan still had one wish left from Omar the genie, wonder what he will wish for next time?...

Facts about the Maldives you might not know.

The traditional food of the Maldives.

3 dishes –

1) Mas Riha – A fish curry typically made with tuna and coconut milk, spices and vegetables.

2) Mas Huni – A popular breakfast dish consisting of tuna coconut onion, lime juice, chilli and salt. Often served with Roti (a flat bread).

3) Gulha – Deep fried pasty balls filled with smoked fish, coconut and onions. Often enjoyed as a snack.

Currency of the Maldives.

The official currency in the Maldives is the rufiyaa which is divided into 100 and 500 rufiyaa. Commonly circulated coins are 10, 25 and 50 lari's.

Traditional outfits / costumes.

The Dhivehi Libaas is the traditional dress for women in the Maldives. It's a long floor-length gown with long sleeves. Particularly worn for ceremonies. Men traditionally wear a Sarong long garment wrapped around their waist.

Language

Maldivian or Dhivehi is the official language of the Maldives. (English is widely spoken).

How many tourists travel to the Maldives each year?

The destination reached a new milestone welcoming 2 million (approximately) visitors each year. With a total of 89,315 from the UK (United Kingdom) and a total of 27,106 from the USA (United States of America).

Do Maldives rely on tourism?

Yes, the economy is primarily dependant on tourism, followed by fishing and shipping. The largest contributor to the Maldivian economy is the tourism industry. They also rely on tuna and agriculture.

Is the Maldives a safe place to travel for tourists?

The Maldives is a safe place to travel with low crime rate. (especially on resort islands).

Hope you enjoyed the Adventures of Nathan and Nyashia.

Never stop learning.

Acknowledgements

I would like to give acknowledgements to the following:

Natalie Mantle

Nyomi Lenny

Callum Williams

Ellexus Mantle

Thanks for the great support that you have given me.

To you, I will always be grateful.

J Lenny.

Dedication

I would like to dedicate this book to my beautiful granddaughter, Ellexus Mantle.

J Lenny.